Pork and Beef's Great Adventure

Written and illustrated by Damon Burnard

Houghton Mifflin Company
Boston 1998

The text of this book is set in 15 point Stone Serif.
The illustrations are gouache on paper.

Library of Congress Cataloging-in-Publication Data

Burnard, Damon.
    Pork and Beef's great adventure / written and illustrated by Damon
Burnard.
        p. cm.
    Summary: One very hot summer, a cow and a pig coat themselves with
frosting and feathers and fly to the moon.
    ISBN 0-395-86765-7
    [1. Cows—Fiction. 2. Pigs—Fiction. 3. Moon—Fiction.
4. Flight—Fiction.] I. Title.
PZ7.B9285Po 1998
[Fic]—dc21   97-8817
                                                                    CIP
                                                                    AC

Manufactured in the United States of America
WOZ 10 9 8 7 6 5 4 3 2 1

This book is dedicated to the inventor of string.
—D.B.

Chapter One

The summer of Pork and Beef's Great
Adventure was so hot, the dogs stopped
chasing the cats and the cats stopped
running from the dogs. Instead, they shook
hands and fried eggs on the sidewalk—that's
how hot it was.

The ground was so dry and cracked, it
looked like a giant brown jigsaw puzzle. And
as for the stream, no one knew quite where it
had gone, but the rumor was that it had gone
there in a hurry, because it left behind its
collection of boots and cans.

And as for Pork and Beef, they spread themselves out like blankets in a shady, gladey, grassy-bladey place, the perfect place on a summer's day: the place beneath the apple tree.

There they stayed the whole day long, until the sun slid slowly away. And then Pork and Beef lay there some more, gazing up through the branches at the velvet, violet sky and the ripe yellow moon that hung there.

"Beef?" said Pork.

"Yes, Pork?" said Beef.

"What's it like on the moon?" asked Pork.

"I really don't know!" said Beef.

"Then why don't we go there tomorrow and find out?" suggested Pork.

"My! What an excellent idea!" agreed Beef, and with that decided, it seemed like the right sort of time to go home to bed.

Chapter Two

In the mornings, Pork and Beef usually awoke to songbirds sweetly singing. But as the summer grew hotter, the birds had mysteriously disappeared. And so on the morning of their Great Adventure, it was an alarm clock that woke them up.

"CLING! CLANG! CLING! CLANG!" it clanged, and Pork and Beef jumped so high out of bed, they bumped their heads on the ceiling. Then off they ran, down to the

kitchen, where they ate their breakfast much too quickly—that's how excited they were.

"Beef?" asked Pork, mopping up milk from the floor. "How exactly are we going to fly to the moon, do you think?"

"I don't know, Pork," said Beef, scrubbing cereal from the walls.

"I don't know, either!" said Pork sadly, and they both stopped what they were doing and teetered on the very brink of Glumness, and Defeat, and Terrible Disappointment.

Suddenly Pork had an idea.

"Hey, Beef!" said Pork. "I've just had an idea," and he whispered it to Beef, who listened with his mouth open, because it was such an excellent idea he completely forgot to close it.

"What an excellent idea, Pork!" said Beef when he'd finished. "And besides, I've always wanted to bathe in frosting!"

Chapter Three

First, Pork and Beef filled the bottom half of the tub with confectioner's sugar and the top half with water. Then they stirred and stirred, and stirred and stirred, until the tub was brimming with beautiful white frosting.

Next, Pork and Beef tiptoed through the house hunting for the biggest, plumpest pillow they could find. And when they found it, they carried it into the bathroom, where they unzipped it and untipped it, until there was a great pile of feathers on the floor.

"You first, Pork!" said Beef.

"No; you first, Beef!" said Pork.

"After you, Pork. I insist!" said Beef. "It was your idea, after all!"

"That's true, Beef," said Pork, "but you did most of the stirring!"

And so it went on, back and forth, until at last they decided to do it together, and with a SPLISH! and a SPLOSH! they jumped into the tub.

In that sticky white deliciousness they splashed about, then out they sprang, onto the feathers, where they rolled around like crazy roly-poly things, until all the feathers had stuck to the frosting, and they were covered from head to toe.

"Ready, Beef?" asked Pork.

"Not quite, Pork!" replied Beef.

"Kitchen, Beef?" asked Pork.

"Kitchen, Pork," said Beef.

And off they went, back to the kitchen, where they found a tin of sardines and a bottle of juice to take with them, in case they got hungry and thirsty.

"Ready, Beef?" asked Pork.

"Ready, Pork!" replied Beef, and off they went, out the front door, to begin their Great Adventure.

Chapter Four

Up to the top of a little round hill walked
Pork and Beef.

"Perfect!" said Beef.

"Ideal!" agreed Pork, and they'd just begun
to flap their arms about when they were
interrupted by the sound of a throat being
cleared.

"Ahem!" said the throat.

When Pork and Beef turned around, they
saw that the throat belonged to Gloomy
Clown.

"Well, well, well!" he remarked. "If it isn't two giant marshmallows!"

"Hee hee!" giggled Pork and Beef. "It's us, Gloomy Clown! Pork and Beef! Covered with feathers and frosting!"

"Oh yes, indeed!" said Gloomy Clown in an unsurprised sort of way. "So it is, so it is . . ."

When Pork and Beef told him about their trip to the moon, Gloomy Clown became less gloomy.

"Oh really?" he sneered. "A flying pig and a flying cow, eh?"

"Of course!" said Beef, as though it were the most natural thing in the world. Which of course it is.

"If you make it to the moon,"
scoffed Gloomy Clown, "I'll tell
you what I'll do; I'll eat my hat, I will.
I'll eat my hat!"

Then off he walked, back down the hill,
cackling all the while like a peculiar kind of
goose.

"It's nice to see Gloomy Clown so cheerful
for a change, isn't it, Beef?" said Pork,
watching him go.

"It certainly is, Pork!" said Beef. "Though I
don't know why he'd want to eat his hat!"

And with that, they went back to their
flapping.

Chapter Five

At first nothing happened.

But then Pork and Beef noticed that their toes were no longer touching the ground, and up they rose, little by little, up into the summer sky.

"WHEEE!" squealed Pork.

"YAHOO!" yelled Beef.

To begin with, they flew in a clumsy, bumpy sort of way. But with a little practice they were soon soaring and swooping like birds, and not like a cow and a pig at all.

"Look!" cried Pork, pointing down. "There's Gloomy Clown!

And there he was, plodding up his path. But he was so busy looking at the ground, he did not see his feathery, frosted friends waving at him.

Higher and higher flew Pork and Beef.

"Beef?" asked Pork after a while. "Where is the moon exactly?" for it was nowhere to be seen.

"I don't know where it is exactly," said Beef, "but I do know the sky's a Big Place. If we keep going up, we're sure to find it!"

And so up and up they flew.

"You know what, Beef?" said Pork, after a time. "All this flying has made me peckish!"

"I'm glad you said that, Pork!" said Beef. "Because I'm feeling a little thirsty!

They looked all about for a Special Place; a place where they could rest for a while. Away in the distance they spied a cloud. It was puffy and white and looked very comfortable indeed.

"Perfect!" Pork exclaimed.

"Ideal!" agreed Beef, and they flapped their way over.

Chapter Six

But when Pork and Beef came down to land on the cloud, they saw to their surprise that they weren't alone.

On its billowy-pillowy whiteness sat a flock of birds.

"Hello, birds!" said Pork and Beef cheerily. But even though the birds returned their greeting, it was plain to see that they were Not Happy Birds. In fact, they were the gloomiest-looking birds that the flying pig and the flying cow had ever seen. And they'd seen a lot.

The birds were as thin as pencils, their
feathers were scraggly, and their beaks were
all bent.

"Oh," said Pork politely. "Have we come at
a bad time?"

"Yes, you have!" a bluebird croaked.

"But then, every time is a bad time nowadays!
It's so hot the stream has dried up, and we
have nothing to drink!"

"Yes!" groaned another. "And the earth is so hard and dry, when we peck for worms, all we get are bent beaks!"

"What's more," moaned another, "the nearest raincloud is still three days away!"

"Three days?" said Beef brightly. "That's not long!"

"Three days is forever!" growled the grumbly bird, to which Beef agreed that without a doubt three days was a very, very long time indeed.

"It's horrible! Horrible!" squawked the
birds, shaking their sad little heads, and Pork
and Beef suddenly realized why they hadn't
been woken by bird song lately.

"Here!" said Pork, reaching into his
feathers. "I brought this little bottle of juice
along! It would make me the happiest pig in
the world if you shared it with us!"

"And here!" joined in Beef. "I brought this little tin of sardines along! It would make me the happiest cow in the world if you shared it with us!"

"Oh, we couldn't!" said the birds.

"Oh, please do!" said Pork and Beef.

"But it's all you have!" said the birds.

"But there's plenty to go around!" insisted Pork and Beef.

And so it went on, back and forth, until at last they all sat down together and had a picnic on that great white cloud, a-sailing through the sky-blue sky.

Chapter Seven

"Phew! I'm full up to here!" said Beef at last, pointing to his neck.

"Well, I'm full up to here!" puffed Pork, pointing a little higher still.

When everyone was just as full as they wanted to be, Beef went around the cloud and cleverly straightened out the birds' beaks with the key from the sardine tin.

All this made the birds very happy indeed. They even agreed that three days didn't seem so long to wait for rain after all.

"How can we ever thank you?" they asked, and Pork and Beef said they could thank them by just carrying on being birds, flying around the sky and singing chirpy little songs and that kind of thing.

"Oh, and we'd be very grateful," said Beef, "if you could please tell us the way to the moon."

The bluebird pointed up, and a little to the left, unless you were looking at him from the other side, in which case he was pointing to the right.

"It's that way!" he said. "You'll see it before too long!"

"Goody!" said Pork.

"Thank you!" said Beef.

And then the bluebird warned them to be careful to start home before sunrise.

"The sun can get very hot when you're that high up," he explained.

Pork and Beef thanked him for the advice and promised to be careful. And with that they dove off the cloud into the great blue sea of sky, and away they flew, up to the moon.

Chapter Eight

"Look, Beef!" cried Pork.

Dusk was falling, and suddenly there it was, hanging behind a silvery cloud.

"Hooray!" said Beef. "We've found the moon!"

The closer Pork and Beef got, the bigger and brighter the moon became.

"It's beautiful!" gushed Pork.

"It's wonderful!" gasped Beef.

Down they glided on their feathery wings, down to land on a little hill, which might have been put there just for them.

"Congratulations, Beef!" said Pork.

"Congratulations, Pork!" said Beef, and they shook hands and hugged each other and felt very happy and glad all over, because they'd done what they said they would and had flown to the moon.

Chapter Nine

There were lots and lots of things for them to do there!

They chased . . .

they hid . . .

they built . . .

and they slid!

Pork and Beef were so busy having fun, they forgot all about the time. And because time goes quickly when you're having fun, before they knew it the great fiery sun was rolling toward them across the sky.

"Look, Pork!" said Beef.

"I see, Beef!" said Pork sadly, because he knew it was time for them to go.

And so they walked back up the hill. They flapped their wings, rose into the air, and started out for home.

And then Pork had an idea.

"Just a minute, Beef!" he cried, and he wheeled around and flapped his way back to the moon.

"What are you doing, Pork?" shouted Beef.

"You'll see!" Pork laughed. He picked up a rock and began to draw in the sand.

"Come on, Pork!" said Beef, who was growing worried because the sun was getting hotter.

"Nearly finished!" said Pork cheerfully. "I'll catch up!" He carried on drawing, and the sun carried on getting hotter.

Chapter Ten

"Please hurry, Pork!" pleaded Beef. "Pork, please hurry!"

"Finished, Beef!" hollered Pork at last. He threw down the rock, ran up the hill, flapped his arms, and rose into the air.

"Phew-ee!" he thought, as he sped down the sky. "It's become awfully, awfully hot!"

And then Pork realized
that it made no difference
whether he flapped or not,
because his frosting was
beginning to melt. And
as it dripped away, with it
went the feathers.

Pork the pig was pink
once more!

A pink Pork, dropping
like a stone!

"Oh dear, Beef!" he said, tumbling over and over. "I'm falling!"

"Don't worry, Pork!" shouted Beef. "I'll catch you!"

And as Pork tumbled down, Beef grabbed him with his hooves.

"Got you, Pork!" laughed Beef.

"Thank you, Beef!" said Pork.

And now the two of them dropped like a stone.

"I'm too heavy, Beef!" said Pork.

"Nonsense, Pork!" scoffed Beef.

"Thank you so very much!" said Pork to the birds, who were the same ones they'd met earlier.

"You're very welcome!" said the birds, bowing graciously.

"How can we ever repay your kindness?" asked Beef. The birds thought for a moment.

"The best way to thank us," they said, "is simply to carry on being Pork and Beef, doing all those things that only Pork and Beef can do!"

"We'll try our best!" said Pork with a bow.

"We will, indeed!" said Beef, and he bowed, too.

And with that decided, they all bowed together one more time and cheerfully bade farewell. Then off flew the birds, back to their cloud. And, as it was getting late, Pork and Beef made their way home.

"Pork?" asked Beef, as they walked along.

"Yes, Beef?" said Pork.

"What exactly were you drawing on the moon?" asked Beef.

"I wasn't drawing," said Pork. "I was writing."

"Oh," said Beef. "And what did you write?"

"You'll just have to wait and see!" said Pork with a little laugh.

"I suppose I will!" chuckled Beef, "I suppose I will!"

Chapter Twelve

That night, as Gloomy Clown sat flossing his teeth in the kitchen, he happened to glance out the window. And out the window he saw the sky, and in the sky he saw the moon, and on the moon he saw some words, and this is what they said:

PORK and Beef weR HeRe!

Gloomy Clown threw back his head and roared with laughter.

He clutched at his sides and wiped tears from his eyes and took his hat from his head and placed it on his plate and sprinkled it with pepper and salt and ate it with a knife and fork. And with every bite he laughed, because Pork and Beef had done what they said they would, and anyway, his hat didn't taste too bad.

Meanwhile, Pork and Beef lay asleep in their beds, dreaming of Wondrous New Adventures . . .